VIKING

THE BATTLE FOR THE VIKING GOLD

Bloomsbury Education
An imprint of Bloomsbury Publishing Plc

50 Bedford Square
London
WC1B 3DP
UK

1385 Broadway
New York
NY 10018
USA

www.bloomsbury.com

First published in 2010 by A & C Black, an imprint of Bloomsbury Publishing Plc

A catalogue record for this book is available from the British Library.

ISBN
PB: 978 1 4729 4211 1
epub: 978 1 4729 5229 5
epdf: 978 1 4729 5227 1

2 4 6 8 10 9 7 5 3 1

Typeset by Newgen Knowledge Works (P) Ltd., Chennai, India

Printed and bound in UK by CPI Group (UK) ltd, Croydon CR0 4YY

TERRY DEARY

VIKING TALES

THE BATTLE FOR THE VIKING GOLD

Inside illustrations by Helen Flook

BLOOMSBURY EDUCATION
AN IMPRINT OF BLOOMSBURY
LONDON OXFORD NEW YORK NEW DELHI SYDNEY

CHAPTER ONE
CANDLE WAX

Whitby, England, 867

"Pass me the candle, Luke," Edwin whispered.

The candle spluttered and sparked. It was made from mutton fat, so it smelled of burnt sheep.

Luke handed the candle holder to his friend. "You wouldn't dare!" he squeaked.

"Watch me," Edwin said.

The boys wore the long, brown robes of monks, which were tied at the waist with rough rope. Edwin pulled up his robe so he could reach forward. The boys were sitting on the balcony in a small church. The monks below were sitting on benches, praying silently.

Edwin looked down on the bald heads; heads that had been scrubbed clear of hair with stones. One day the boys would have their heads scrubbed that way.

Edwin moved along so that the candle was on the edge of the wooden rail in front of him. "That's Brother James below me now," he said.

"You wouldn't dare!" Luke squeaked again.

Edwin tilted the candle. A fat blob of wax dropped off the end. It hit the bench

below and cooled to a hard yellow ball in the chilly air.

The young monk moved the candle along. He let the flame melt a little more wax, and then tilted it forward again. This time, the hot wax fell straight towards the bald patch on the head of Brother James, and struck him, still warm and soft.

The old monk didn't move. His eyes stayed closed. His lips still moved in prayer.

Edwin choked back a giggle and Luke dragged him out of his seat. He pulled his friend down the stairs and out onto the path by the church.

"You're mad," Luke moaned. "He'll beat you."

"No, he won't," Edwin said.

"He will."

"I'll tell him it was *you* that did it," Edwin laughed, and ran off to the refectory to eat.

The boys found some lamb knucklebones in the kitchen. They were neat cubes and perfect for a game of chuck-stones. The young monks played for a while.

Slowly, the refectory filled with the monks returning from the church. The cook brought out pots of fish and oatmeal porridge. The abbot was first to be served, and then the monks. Finally, the novices – the boys – held out their plates.

The monks ate in silence. But when Edwin held out his plate, a harsh voice said,

"No, Edwin does not want to eat today."

The boys looked up to see Brother James standing at the end of the table. He was a tall, thin man with a face as hard as the cliffs at the edge of the abbey.

"Novice Edwin is at the monastery so he can pray. The fishermen and farmers in Whitby town work hard so they can eat.

Our work is praying. Edwin did not pray today, so Edwin will not eat," the old monk said.

"I did!" Edwin cried.

"I said *pray* not play. You chose to play at dripping candle wax onto the heads of the monks. Your first punishment is to have no food today. Your second punishment is to sit at the table and watch the others eat. And your third punishment is to spend the afternoon in the new field at the top of the cliffs. You will start clearing away the stones. You will fill ten sacks with stones before you eat again."

Luke clutched at his mouth to smother a giggle.

Brother James glared at him. "Did I say something funny, Novice Luke?"

"No, Brother James."

"No. If I see you laughing at your friend's

punishment, then you will join him. There are many, many stones waiting to be cleared before we can plant cabbages there. Now eat."

"Yes, Brother James."

CHAPTER TWO
HANDS

As the sun set in the west, Edwin filled his last sack. He dragged it to the walls of the monastery and sank to the ground. A bell rang in the church tower. It was calling the monks to evening prayers – vespers. Edwin was too tired and weak to rise.

A shadow fell over him, and he looked up to see Brother James.

"Are you ready to eat now, Edwin?"

"What about vespers?"

"I said that praying is our work. Stone picking has been your work today, so you do not need to pray this evening. Let me help you up." The old monk reached down and took Edwin's hand.

The boy gave a sharp cry.

"What is wrong?" the monk asked. He turned the boy's hands so the palms faced upwards. They were scratched and bruised from the stones. "Let's go to the infirmary and bandage those hands," the old man said. His voice was now as soft as the sand on Whitby beach.

As he rubbed ointment into Edwin's palms, he said, "One day, your hands will be hard as mine."

"Did you get hard hands from picking stones?" Edwin asked.

"No, I got them from handling swords and shields," the monk explained, as he wrapped clean linen around the wounds.

"You were a soldier?"

"I was a soldier," Brother James nodded. "But in the end you grow tired of the killing, the fighting, the anger and the fury. In the end, you want peace."

"Did you kill many men?" Edwin whispered.

"I tried not to," Brother James said and the candle-shadow lines on his face were as deep as furrows on a ploughed field. "When the Vikings came, we had to fight to save our villages."

"But you gave up in the end?" Edwin said.

"The Vikings tell tales. They love stories about their gods. Of course it is nonsense. There is only one god – our god. But some of their stories are wise."

"You know Viking stories?" Edwin asked.

"I remember one story that a very old Viking told me. I beat him in battle, but he laughed as I held my sword to his neck. He said there was one enemy none of us could beat."

"A monster? One of their trolls? A giant?"

The Viking told me the tale of the god they call Thor. They say he is the god of Thunder. Thor was the greatest warrior the world had ever seen."

"But he met a greater warrior?"

"Wait, young Edwin. You cannot hurry a good story."

"Sorry," the boy mumbled.

"One day, Thor met an old woman in a Viking hall. Her name was Elli. She said Thor must wrestle with her if he wanted to leave. Thor laughed. He walked to the door. He didn't want to wrestle with an old woman."

"Brave men don't fight against the old and the weak," Edwin nodded.

"But Elli wouldn't let him leave the hall. When he tried to push past her, she grabbed hold of him and started to wrestle. Of course he had to wrestle himself free."

"And he beat her."

"Oh no," Brother James said. "Oh no, he didn't."

CHAPTER THREE
WRESTLING

Brother James went on with his story. "Old Elli looked as twisted as an ancient tree. But old trees can be tougher than iron. The more Thor struggled, the stronger the old woman became."

"She was a witch," Edwin guessed.

"Let me finish the tale," Brother James said. "Thor gathered all his strength. He locked hands with Elli and twisted until she went down on one knee. The crowd in the hall cheered."

"Why? Because he was beating an old woman?"

"Wait and see... Thor struggled on, but he couldn't throw her to the floor. Slowly, his strength went and Elli pulled Thor to one knee, too. And there they stayed. Neither able to overthrow the other. In the end, they agreed it was a draw."

"Thor isn't much of a god if he couldn't wrestle an old woman," Edwin said with a sniff.

"Ah, but after the fight was over, the men in the hall told Thor the truth. No one had ever beaten Elli. Not since time began. For Elli was Old Age itself. And none of us can ever beat old age."

Edwin sat silent for a while. "I see what you mean. It's a wise tale. And old age made you a monk?"

Brother James smiled a wintry smile. "Old age and good sense. There is only one way to beat the Vikings – with a prayer book in our hand, not a sword. When they give up their cruel old gods and follow our god, then there will be peace."

"The Vikings raided Hartlepool Abbey last week. They could attack us here at any time," young Edwin said. "Are you saying that if the Vikings come to Whitby, you'll fight them with a prayer book?"

"Time for supper," Brother James said, and led the way across the abbey lawns.

The next morning, Edwin was given an easier job – collecting shellfish on the shore below the cliffs. As he reached into the rock pools, the salt stung his raw hands, but helped to heal them.

"Ships!" came a voice from the cliff top. Edwin looked up and saw Luke pointing out to sea. "Come and see them!" he cried.

Edwin ran up the steep cliff path with his basket and joined his friend.

"Three ships," Luke said happily. "They are traders come to sell their goods. The abbot will buy their French wines and their spices. We will eat and drink well this week."

Edwin squinted into the morning sun. "Traders have ships as round as the moon... they call them knorrs. The ships heading this way are long and narrow.

They're just big enough to carry two dozen men and their weapons."

"Weapons?" Luke squawked. "You mean they're Viking warriors?"

"I think so," Edwin said.

"What can we do?" Luke cried.

"Fight," Edwin said.

"What do we fight them with?" Luke wailed.

"Prayer books, Luke," Edwin replied.

CHAPTER FOUR
RUNNING

Edwin's sandals hardly touched the turf as he raced along the cliff top to the abbey. "Vikings!" he cried. "Vikings!"

The abbot came to the door of his room, red-faced and fearful. "We are lost! Oh, we are lost! Lord have mercy on us!"

But old Brother James strode across the lawn

and stood on the steps of the church. From the top step he called out, "Let us make ready!"

The monks gathered around to listen.

Brother James spoke quickly and calmly. "How far from shore, Edwin?"

"About half an hour," the boy panted.

"They will want to steal the valuables from the church," the old monk said.

"So let's hide them," the abbot moaned.

"If we do that, they will know. They will torture you to find out where they are. It's best to hide *half* of them and let them take the other half. Then they will be happy."

"A much better idea," the abbot nodded.

"Simon and Peter, take the silver crosses from the chapels and put them on the cliff top. Then find the ten sacks of stones by the gate and pile them on top of the silver. The Vikings will think it is a marker on the cliff top for the fisherman to find their way home. Leave the gold cross on the main altar. They can have it."

"The gold cross," the abbot gasped. "Not the gold cross!"

Brother James looked grim. "The gold cross... or torture."

"The gold cross," the abbot said.

"Now, young Luke. I want you to run into town and tell the people to flee to the hills. Tell them to take what they can carry, and let the Vikings have the rest. Then join them. The Vikings won't want to go too far from their boats. We'll ring the church bell when it's safe to return."

"You want me to run away?" Luke said.

"You and Edwin. The Vikings want young men for slaves. If they see you, they'll take you with them. They won't bother with the old ones. Well? What are you waiting for? Run!"

Luke turned and sped through the abbey gate into the town.

Edwin hung back. "Will you be all right, Brother James?" he asked.

The monk shrugged. "I am old. I have lived a good life. If the Vikings don't get me, then Elli will. No one can beat old age. Now go!"

Edwin backed away slowly. "You will fight them with your prayer book?"

Brother James nodded. "God be with you, boy," he said.

"God be with you," Edwin said.

The old monk gave a thin smile. "I hope God remembers to bring a very large shield."

CHAPTER THREE KNUCKLEBONES

When the Vikings landed, they found the town of Whitby empty. The people had fled, carrying their valuables with them.

The Vikings smashed down some of the doors and stuffed themselves with food the townsfolk had left behind.

Their leader, Snorri, blew a hunting horn and called them back to the ship. "It's a poor fishing town," he said. "The only riches will be in that abbey up on the cliff top. Follow me."

The gates to the abbey stood open. The old monks moved slowly around the gardens or worked in the scriptorium, copying books.

The gardeners looked up and stood quietly as the Vikings charged in.

The abbot stepped out to greet them. He tried to say, "Can I help you, my friends?" But his lips turned to whale blubber and his tongue to calf's-foot jelly. He said, "Cabble ip plah, fuh-fuh truh?"

Snorri scowled at him. He drew his sword. "I can kill you now, or you can tell me where your treasures are."

"Cabble ip plah, fuh-fuh truh?"

It was Brother James who stepped forward and smiled gently at the tip of the sword. "We are a poor monastery..."

"Ahhhh!" Snorri roared. "I *knew* you would say that. How did I know you would say that? Because they *all* say that," he sneered.

The Viking warriors laughed.

Snorri nodded to them, and some of them set out to search the abbey.

"We have silver candlesticks and a gold cross at the altar," the old monk called after them helpfully. "Please take them. We will make a simple wooden cross. And every day, when you look at our golden cross, you can think of our god and remember how good he is."

Snorri frowned. "Uh? We have our own gods."

Brother James nodded slowly. "Do they give you golden crosses?"

"Well... no... but..."

"Then please take ours. Our god would want you to have it."

"He would?"

"Oh, yes," Brother James said, and he opened the prayer book he was carrying. "Blessed are the poor, he says. If you make us poor, then you make us *blessed*, see?"

"And if I slice off your head at your wrinkled neck?"

"Then I shall die poor and will go to heaven, brother."

"You are mad... *brother*," Snorri spat.

The warriors came back to the garden carrying some pieces of silver and the gold cross.

Snorri sneered at them. "Not enough. We have travelled a long way to make you poor and blessed. If you have no more riches, then we'll take the young ones for slaves."

"Young ones?" Brother James said. "There are no young ones here in the monastery," he said.

He was telling the truth.

"There are always young ones," Snorri said quietly. One of his warriors walked up to his leader and opened his hand. In his palm were five lamb knucklebones.

"We played that game as boys," Snorri said. "Old monks don't play chuck-stones. Tell me where your boys are, or I will shut you all in the church and set fire to it. Then we will destroy the town – burn it so fiercely that the ashes will blow away and leave nothing. Nothing, old monk. All for the sake of a few boy slaves. Would you want that? Well? Where are they?"

CHAPTER SIX
SLAVES

"Slaves," Edwin groaned. He lay on the sheep-cropped grass of the hills. "The Vikings will want to take home slaves."

"Well, they're not getting me," Luke muttered.

Edwin raised his head and looked over the ridge of the hill to the town below. "They will be angry."

"Serves them right."

"No. Think, Luke. If they are angry, they will take revenge. They could burn down the abbey or start killing our brothers."

"The brothers that punished you," Luke argued.

"The brothers that showed me I was a foolish child to drip candle wax on an old man's head. It was a lesson, Luke. We may make fun of the old monks, but they are good men... better than the cruel Vikings. We have to help."

Luke turned red with shame. "I know... but we can't stop them."

"We can make them less angry," Edwin argued. "We must go back to the monastery. Let them take us."

Luke shivered. "No. They may kill us."

"So? If they don't kill us, then old age will – have you heard the story of Elli? I'm going back."

"You're mad!" Luke wailed. "You'll die."

"That's true," Edwin laughed, and rose to his feet.

"Wait for me," Luke groaned.

The two young monks walked bravely down the hillside towards the abbey. The grass was springy under their sandals.

"They don't have grass like this in Norway," Luke sighed. "They say it's all mountains and rocks."

"So, we pick rocks for the Vikings. It's just like picking rocks for Brother James."

"You won't be saying that when they order you to pick a mountain," Luke grumbled.

Edwin laughed.

As they entered the gates, they saw a

group of Viking warriors start to push the old monks towards the church. One Viking seemed to be in charge. He held a flaming log of wood that he had plucked from the kitchen fire.

"Your last chance, old man," the Viking leader said to Brother James. "Where are the boys?"

"We're here," Edwin said.

The Viking turned slowly and a grin spread over his face. "So you are. So you are. Welcome, my young friends. How would you like to make a little trip over the seas?"

Edwin and Luke stood silent. The Viking walked over to them slowly and gripped the hoods of their robes, one in each hand. He lifted them off their feet. "Skinny, but you'll sell well in the markets of Stafangr."

He turned towards the gates of the abbey, dragging the boys with him. But a figure blocked his path. It was Brother James.

"I cannot let you take the boys," he said.

Snorri blinked. "Cannot? *Cannot?* Who is going to stop me?"

"I am," Brother James said.

CHAPTER SEVEN
PRAYER BOOK

Snorri looked around at the Viking warriors. Some of the monks peered around the church door to see what would happen next.

“I am a Viking,” Snorri said in a rumbling voice. “I do not want to hurt an old man who has lost half his wits.”

“Good,” Brother James smiled. “I do not want to hurt you, either.”

Snorri took a deep breath to hold back his rage. He put down the two boys and looked at one of his fair-haired warriors. “Get him out of my way,” he ordered.

The warrior strolled over to the old monk. He stretched out an arm to grab him by the shoulder. What followed happened so quickly that no one was quite sure what Brother James did. He seemed to pull the warrior towards him. As the surprised man stumbled forwards, Brother James rolled onto his back, placed a foot in the warrior's stomach and sent him flying like a Whitby gull. The Viking stopped flying when he hit the garden wall, and there he lay, groaning.

Snorri squinted hard at Brother James as the old man rose to his feet. "Are you a soldier? You fight like one."

"I am a monk," the old man shrugged, and dusted down his robe carefully.

"Only soldiers can fight like that," Snorri argued.

Brother James thought about this for a while. "Elli wasn't a soldier, was she? She was just an old woman. But she stopped Thor from leaving the hall, didn't she?"

"Yes, but Elli had magical powers. She had old age on her side," the Viking said.

"I have old age on *my* side," Brother James said. "And my magical power comes from this." He reached into a pocket and pulled out his prayer book.

"Your books can't stop iron weapons," the Viking raged. He reached into his belt and swept his sword from it.

Brother James stood still.

Suddenly Edwin ran to the fair-haired warrior, who was still lying by the wall. He tore the dazed man's sword away and threw it towards the old monk.

"Fight, Brother James, fight!"

Snorri gave a roar. He stepped forward and brought his sword down in a terrible sweep towards the old man's skull.

Brother James raised his sword to meet the blow. His thin arm, wrinkled, twisted and as strong as an ancient tree, stayed firm. The swords clashed with a clang that rang around the monastery like the church bell.

"I won't be beaten by an old man like you," Snorri screamed.

"That's what Thor probably said," the monk laughed.

CHAPTER EIGHT
VIKING IRON

Snorri the Viking threw himself at Brother James. But every stroke the Viking made was met with the firm sword of the monk.

The other monks came out of the church.

"Pray, brothers, pray!" the abbot cried.

The men fell to their knees and raised their eyes to the sky.

"Asking your gods for help?" Snorri whined. "That's cheating."

In his rage, the Viking chief raised his weapon high above his head and brought it crashing down in a blow that would split a man from head to waist. But when Storri's sword met the monk's, it snapped in two.

The Vikings gasped. The monks stopped praying.

"Kill the monk before he kills me," Snorri ordered his men.

A warrior stepped forwards. "No, Snorri. You cannot defeat old age. Even Thor was beaten by Elli. Leave him. Let's go home."

The warriors muttered among themselves and started to head for the gates. Snorri followed slowly. The boys and the silver were left behind.

The Viking looked at the old monk. "You didn't beat me... not by yourself," he said.

"No," Brother James agreed. "I had the help of my god."

"He must be a great god... greater than Thor."

"He is," the abbot said, bustling forwards.

"Our god will always beat your gods, so go on – clear off."

Snorri looked angry and waved the broken stump of his sword at the abbot.

The abbot jumped backwards and cried, "Keep away from me, you bully. Go away and stay away!"

"Tell your people what happened," Brother James said. "Then come back. Come back and we will tell you *our* stories."

Snorri shook his head. He wandered out of the gate and back towards the ships.

"That was so brave," Luke said to Brother James.

The old man threw down the sword, wearily. "No. Not brave. Fighting steel with steel isn't brave. What you and Edwin did was brave. If you hadn't come back, they would have killed us all. You came back with no swords and no hope. You risked your freedom to help your brothers."

Edwin stayed silent.

Brother James smiled and the winter in his face showed shades of summer. "It's like the abbot said, our god will always beat their gods... at least so long as there are heroes like you. Let's go and eat," he said.

Luke grinned. "Yes, being a hero is hungry work."

EPILOGUE

The Danes attacked and burned Whitby in 867 CE. The monastery was so badly damaged that the monks didn't return until 1078. In the battle of beliefs, though, it was the Viking gods who lost.

In time, the fighting gods like Thor were forgotten. The Vikings settled in England and became farmers, not fighters – and many of them also became Christians. Monasteries like Whitby were smashed, but the spirit of the monks wasn't destroyed.

In every monastery, there were all sorts of people. There were even boys like Edwin and Luke – and dripping candle wax onto monks' bald heads really was one of the tricks they played!

Not all the people in the monasteries were good men. A monk called Alcuin said many monks led such bad lives that they deserved to be attacked by Vikings. He wrote an angry letter, saying, "Think, brothers – maybe this curse arrived because of your evil ways. Look at the rich clothes, the proud way you wear your hair, the rich feasts of the princes and people." Can you imagine being attacked because of your haircut?

The monasteries went on for another 600 years, until an English king, Henry VIII, closed them down. He grabbed their land and their money for himself. If any monks tried to stop him, they were hanged from the church steeples.

The Vikings robbed and ruined a few monasteries in Britain – but a cruel king robbed and ruined them all.

YOU TRY

1. My monastery

Monks wanted monasteries to be their own villages. Imagine you are one of a group of monks. The local lord has given you some land for a monastery of your own. (You will pray for him – not pay him!)

Plan your monastery. There is a river close by, and a small wood. Remember you have to feed yourselves, heat and light the buildings, and do your holy work – copying prayer books, for example. You will certainly need somewhere to pray and somewhere to sleep. What else will you need?

2. Monks' monasteries

When you have planned your monastery, do some research and find plans of real-life monasteries. Use books or the internet to find out what the monks of old built.

Did you forget anything in your plan? Or did the monks miss anything that you would have added?

Terry Deary Saxon Tales

Find more fantastically fun (and sometimes gory) adventures in Terry Deary's Saxon Tales. Based on real historical events!